© 1997 Owl Records Ltd
Published by Geddes & Grosset,
David Dale House, New Lanark, ML11 9DJ, Scotland,
for Owl Records Ltd, Dublin, Ireland

First printed 1997
Reprinted 1999, 2000, 2002

ISBN 1 85534 770 9

Printed and bound in Slovenia

Etain and Midir

Illustrated by Heather McKay

Tarantula Books

E tain was a very happy child. She had soft golden hair and clear blue eyes.

She loved to play in the forest and to swim in the sea. She loved to sit on the cliffs, watching the waves roll in and roll out again. She loved to hear the wind whisper her name, "Etain — Etain."

Most of all, she loved dreaming her dreams.

Her favourite dream was of a fair-haired, handsome prince. She dreamt that he would take her away on a white horse to a land where no one ever grew old.

Etain grew up to become the most beautiful young woman in all Ireland.

One day, a tall, dark stranger on a black horse came riding by.

The stranger was Eochy, King of Ireland. As soon as Eochy saw Etain, he fell in love with her.

Day after day, he returned to watch Etain playing in the fields and in the forest.

After a few weeks, Eochy asked Etain to marry him. She agreed. Soon she became Queen of Ireland.

The wedding feast lasted seven days and seven nights. The whole of Ireland rejoiced.

Eochy built a beautiful castle for Etain.

The castle had three hundred and sixty five windows, one for each day of the year. The walls were covered with wonderful paintings. The floors were covered with soft red carpets.

Every night in the castle there was music, dancing and story telling.

At first, Etain was happy. She had everything she had dreamed of.

T hen one night, a storyteller told the story of Tír na nÓg.

He told them that Tír na nÓg was a magical land where no one ever grew old.

He told them of a fair-haired prince called Midir.

He told them of Midir's beautiful princess, called Etain.

He said Etain had disappeared without a trace from Tír na nÓg.

E tain suddenly remembered her dreams. Slowly she began to realise that she was the beautiful princess who had disappeared from Tír na nÓg.

   She remembered that a wicked fairy had cast a spell on her. She remembered how the fairy had turned her into a moth. She remembered being blown on the wind across the seas to Ireland.

S uddenly, Etain realised that before she was born, she had lived in Tír na nÓg.

From then on, Etain became very unhappy. She longed to go back to Tír na nÓg. Once more she could hear voices on the wind calling her name, "Etain — Etain."

One night, the wind was very strong and the voices were very loud.

E tain looked through her bedroom window.

Out on the hillside, she saw a fair-haired handsome prince on a white horse.

Etain knew that this was the prince from her dreams. She knew that this was Midir, who had come to take her back to Tír na nÓg.

When Eochy saw the stranger, he was afraid. He feared that Midir would take Etain away from him.

He called out all of his armies. He gave orders that the palace was to be guarded by seven hundred warriors. All the doors and windows of the palace were locked.

Eochy gave orders for Etain to be locked in the dungeon.

The dungeon was dark and cold. Etain was very unhappy. She cried and prayed that Midir would come and rescue her.

The wind blew stronger and stronger. The voice grew louder and louder, "Etain — Etain."

Even deep in the dungeon, Etain could hear the wind.

Suddenly, it all stopped.

A bright light shone into the dark dungeon.

As if by magic, Midir appeared out of the darkness. He took Etain into his arms.

Immediately, they turned into two white swans.

Outside, Eochy and the soldiers were frightened. They saw the roof of the dungeon open up. Then they saw two white swans fly out through the open roof.

The soldier watched the swans fly off into the distance. Then the two swans disappeared.

Midir and Etain had gone back to Tír na nÓg. That is where they still live today in perfect happiness.